Other Books by John Hawksinson

COLLECT, PRINT AND PAINT FROM NATURE

MORE TO COLLECT AND PAINT FROM NATURE

OUR WONDERFUL WAYSIDE

THE OLD STUMP

ROBINS AND RABBITS

WINTER TREE BIRDS

Where the Wild Apples Grow

Story and Pictures by
JOHN HAWKINSON

Albert Whitman & Company   Chicago

© 1967 Albert Whitman & Company
L.C. Catalog Card Number 67-17418
Published Simultaneously in Canada
by George J. McLeod, Ltd., Toronto
Printed in the United States of America

84170

High up on a pale hill
there lived a beautiful white horse.
He belonged to no one,
and no one belonged to him.

Below him there was a dark forest.

Small dark animals lived there.
Not very many. Not very friendly.

And below the dark forest
there was a little valley
where the sun shone
and the wild apples grew.

And in a cave near the valley
where the wild apples grew
there lived a little girl
with long brown hair.
She belonged to no one,
and no one belonged to her.

In the fall, when the moon
was bright and yellow,
the horse from the pale green hill
would run through the dark forest.

He ran to the little valley
where the wild apples grew.
And he stood in the moonlight
and ate ripe, red apples.
From the cave, the girl
with the long brown hair
watched in wonder and delight.

In another valley, pretty far away,
there was a little town.
In the town there were cats, dogs,
children, and people.
The cats belonged to themselves.
But the dogs belonged to the children,
the children belonged to the people,
and the people belonged
to the singing club,
to the town council,
to the chess club,
to the sewing circle,
to the band —
to clubs for this
and clubs for that.

The people in their clubs made lots of
important decisions and filed them away
in boxes marked "For Further Study."

A river ran right past the town.
It had a very old stone bridge over it.
Every Sunday afternoon in the spring and summer,
everyone went fishing from the bridge.

In October, when the hills turned red and gold,
the dogs, the children, and all the people
went mushrooming in the woods.

They all carried baskets—even the dogs.

Everyone found mushrooms.
They filled all the baskets.
Of course the dogs couldn't
pick mushrooms, so the children
filled baskets for them.

Naturally the people
knew just the right ones
to pick, for they had
all picked mushrooms before,
and were still alive.

The sun was high in the sky. The baskets were full.
The people saw a little valley with soft green grass
and some wild apple trees.
"My, what a wonderful place to have a picnic before
we go home," someone said.
"Yes, yes, let's have a picnic here,"
all the children cried.
So the people sat down and brought out
the bread, the cheese, the sausage,
and the cookies. They ate and ate.

After such a big picnic, everyone became drowsy.
So they fell asleep—dogs, children, and people.
No one was awake to see the sun disappear behind a cloud
or hear the rustle of the leaves in the wind.

But high on the pale green hill the thunder roared,
lightning flashed, and the rain came down in torrents.
The beautiful white horse ran from his home,
through the dark forest, and down to the valley
where the wild apples grew.

The storm came to the valley.
The people woke up. The dogs barked.
The children cried.
Baskets and belongings were snatched up.
Apples flew from the trees. Everyone looked for shelter.
"Look," a man shouted. "See the rocks over there!"
And everyone ran to the rocks on the side of the valley.

A boy who could run very fast
got there first and shouted back to the others,
"Over here, over here—I see a cave!"

Everyone stood at the entrance to the cave
and watched the rain come down—
all except a boy who went exploring back in the cave.

He soon ran back to his father. "Come with me,"
he said. "I think there's something in the cave."
His father asked the people to be quiet, and he talked
to the men in whispers.
The men got together and
walked slowly back in the cave
until their feet
touched some leaves.
"Strike a light.
Let's see what it is,"
a man whispered.

"Look, it's a little girl!"
"Wonder who she belongs to?"
"Shhh, she's asleep."

And it was the little girl with the long brown hair
asleep in her nest of leaves and milkweed down.

The men called the women and children. They all came
except one small child, who was so busy watching the storm
that she didn't hear.
The little cave girl woke up and saw
all the people standing by her nest.

Before anyone could say a word, she darted through the crowd and out of the cave.

The people rushed back to the entrance of the cave.

The small child who stayed to watch the storm met them with arms waving.

"I saw a girl with long brown hair. I saw a beautiful white horse. They went away," she said.

The child looked far off. "Where is she going? Is she going home?"

"Yes, I think so," said her mother.

"Was she riding the horse?" asked a man.

"Yes, I think so," replied the small child.

Everyone wondered where the strange girl's home was.

The rain stopped.
The sun came out again.
The people went home,
and the valley where
the wild apples grew was quiet.

Just as the sun was about to go down,
the horse that lived on the pale green hill
came back to the valley.
He nibbled some grass near an apple tree.
And from her cave, the little girl with
the long brown hair watched in wonder and delight.

Date Due

FE 20	FEB 11	MR 02 '84	
MR 3	FE 13 '78	OC 9 '84	
AP 11	Spec. Special		
	Bennett 1485		
Oc 17	McNeal		
De 12	MY 31 78		
Je 16	MR 27 79		
	MY 12 '79		
Jl 15	JY 11 79		
SEP 9	NO 11 '81		
OCT 8			
Judy Coole			
Feb. 16, 71			
OCT 21	AP 15 '81		
OCT 17	JA 24 '83		
MAR 31	JE 28 '83		
OCT 27 1973			